Walt Disney's
AMERICAN CLASSICS
Davy Crockett

Twin Books

MALLARD
PRESS

D1120068

Davy Crockett was born long ago on a mountain top in Tennessee, the greenest state in the land. His ma and pa were very proud of their little one.

Even as a young boy Davy believed in fair play. Once a bully was picking on a smaller kid. Davy teased the bully and a chase began. As the bully came after him, Davy hid and the bully ran headlong into a whole pack of skunks!

Part of growing up on the frontier meant being good with a rifle, so when he grew old enough Davy entered a shooting match against mean and nasty Big Foot Mason, the best shot in Tennessee.

Big Foot scored one bull's eye and then he put his second bullet only about an inch from bull's eye. Davy's first shot hit the bull's eye dead center, and then he put his second shot in the same hole!
Davy won the match, easily!

After he lost, Big Foot Mason ran off as fast as his big feet would carry him. From that point, the legend of Davy Crockett began to spread far and wide!

Davy gave the prize he had won for shooting—a big milk cow—to the poorest family in town. Not only was Davy becoming a legend, but he was becoming the kind of fellow that folks liked to know!

As a friendly fellow, Davy liked to smile, but when he really set to grinning, he could grin down almost any critter in the forest.

One day he started grinning at a raccoon. The raccoon stared, and Davy grinned until the raccoon became so confused he jumped right out of his skin and ran off naked.

That's how Davy got the coonskin cap that he always wore.

Not only did Davy grin down that old raccoon, he once grinned down a big old bear that had been bothering folks.

The bear stood there—and Davy stood there. Then Davy started grinning, and after a while that big old bear just rolled over a-tremblin, with his paws stuck straight out.

Davy took pity and let him go, but nobody ever saw that pesky bear again.

Sometimes when his grin wasn't good enough, Davy had to use his rifle.

One day Davy was attacked by a mountain lion *and* a bear! Quickly Davy fired a bullet at the point of a rock between the two. The bullet split and hit both of them!

Down they went, howling for mercy. They were really more embarrassed than hurt and Davy let them go. He was the only person in history to pardon a mountain lion and a bear at the same time.

Davy grew up to become a legendary scout in the Tennessee woods. The big animals had learned to respect him and the smaller animals seemed to know that he was their friend.

Folks often talked about Davy's amazing powers. Not only could he grin down a bear, but they told of one morning so cold that the sun froze tight and couldn't rise! It seemed the sun was stuck inside a big snowball, and everywhere Davy looked there was ice, ice and more ice. Even the critters of the woods were iced up.

Davy grabbed a pail of hot grease and poured it around the sun.

Sure enough, at daybreak the next day, the sun thawed enough to rise.

It wasn't but a few weeks afterward that there came the news that a comet was about to crash into Tennessee. Davy ran to the top of the highest mountain and waited.

As the comet flew in just over his head, Davy latched onto its tail and twirled it like a gigantic lasso. With a whoop, he flung that comet right back into outer space where it came from!

21

Along about that time, there was an Indian uprising on the frontier. Colonel Andy Jackson of the US Army called on Davy and his friends, the Tennessee Volunteers, to help out. Davy not only knew the territory as well as any Indian, but he knew their habits and methods of attack.

Davy agreed to help and came across an Army troop that was under attack by Creek Indians. He and two of his volunteer friends rode back into the thick brush, and when Davy yelled, "Charge!" he and his friends began whooping and banging on trees so much they each sounded like a whole troop themselves!

At the sound of the racket, the Creeks thought the whole US Army had arrived, and just plain skedaddled.

In time, Davy helped make peace with the Indians. He respected them, and he often visited his Creek friends when the war was over. He even went to Congress to make sure that the peace treaties were being upheld.

The Indians knew that Davy could be trusted, for Davy Crockett was a man of his word.

It was about this time that Davy met a fellow named George Russell. Before long the two became best friends and over the years, they enjoyed many adventures together.

For instance, one evening after George had been playing his guitar, they went fishing together. By accident George fell into the river, his guitar still strapped around his neck.

When Davy hauled him to the bank, out of the guitar jumped a catfish, a couple of crawdads and a bullfrog!

Now that the Indian uprising was over and things were peaceful, Davy and George decided to say farewell to their friends in Tennessee and head out West to explore the wide-open spaces.

It was a great land—just the sort of place that suited men like Davy and George. It was full of the kind of wide-open spaces they loved. For weeks they didn't see any other people, and they began to think they were the only people on the Frontier.

That is, until one morning…

... as they were about to put their breakfast on the campfire, a trader rushed up to them. He pleaded for their help, saying that a small handful of Americans were going to fight the whole Mexican Army at a fort down in Texas called the Alamo.

Davy and George knew that they must go there at once.

When they arrived at the Alamo, Davy met a man from Arkansas named Jim Bowie. Jim was becoming famous for a big knife he had invented, which was tough enough to chop down a tree. To this day folks still call it the "Bowie knife."

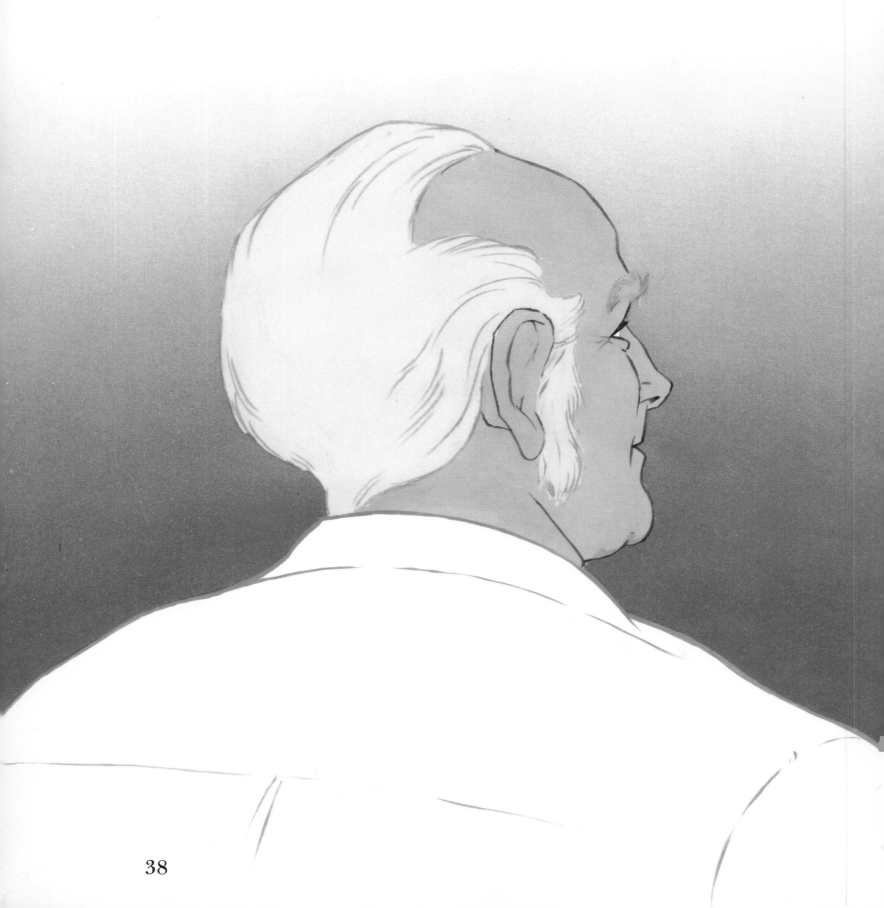

All too soon it was time to fight the Mexican Army who wanted to take over Texas. Davy Crockett, George Russell, Jim Bowie and a number of other brave souls prepared to defend the Alamo and the people of Texas.

While the Alamo itself was just a little fort near the Rio Grande River, that battle meant a lot to people who believed in freedom.

Well, Davy and his friends fought courageously to the last man. What they did at the Alamo was so inspiring that the people of Texas *did* eventually defeat the Mexican Army, and won the right to be part of the United States.

Folks still tell the stories of Davy's heroic deeds. Wherever the critters frisk about in the forest, or a breeze glides down a grassy valley, the spirit of Davy Crockett lives on.

The courage, determination and love of freedom that Davy Crockett stood for are the same things that America stands for today.

First published in the United States of America in 1989 by The Mallard Press.

Mallard Press and its accompanying design and logo are trademarks of BDD Promotional Book Company, Inc.
Produced by Twin Books
15 Sherwood Place
Greenwich, CT 06830

ISBN 0-792-45054-X

Designed, edited and illustrated by
American Graphic Systems, San Francisco

Printed in Hong Kong in 1990